Nina
Fairy Ballerina

Party Magic

Anna Wilson

Illustrated by Nicola Slater

MACMILLAN CHILDREN'S BOOKS

First published 2007 by Macmillan Children's Books
a division of Macmillan Publishers Limited
20 New Wharf Road, London N1 9RR
Basingstoke and Oxford
www.panmacmillan.com

Associated companies throughout the world

ISBN: 978-0-330-44778-2

1 3 5 7 9 8 6 4 2

A CIP catalogue record for this book is available from
the British Library.

Typeset by Nigel Hazle
Printed and bound in Great Britain by Mackays of Chatham plc, Kent

For Felix Horatio Dominic Lazell,
born 27 September 2006.
With love from Auntie Anna
                                    ✗✗✗

Chapter One

Nina was not her usual chirpy self. Her favourite teacher, Miss Tremula, had recently announced her intention to retire, and Nina didn't know what she would do without her. In an attempt to cheer up their friend, Peri and Bella suggested they ask Madame Dupré if they could help organize the leaving party. It was to be an extra-special occasion, as Miss Tremula was going to be one hundred years old on the day she left the Academy.

"Don't worry, Nina," Peri said,

fluttering alongside her. "I'm sure Miss Tremula will stay in touch. After all, you are her star pupil."

"Yeah, stop moping!" Bella teased, linking her arm through Nina's. "Just think about how exciting it will be on Miss T's birthday. I can't believe she's a hundred!"

Peri giggled. "I always thought my granny was old, but Miss T's *ancient* – not

that you'd know it," she added hastily, seeing the look on Nina's face. "She's such a graceful ballerina."

Nina nodded. "I'm sorry, guys. I'm just going to miss her so much!"

"Maybe our new teacher will be even better," Peri said encouragingly, as the fairies knocked and went into the office.

Nina was about to protest that *no one* could be better than Miss Tremula when she was almost knocked over by a very flustered Miss Meadowsweet. Nina was alarmed at the look of panic on the secretary's face.

"I'm *so* sorry!" Miss Meadowsweet cried, as papers, pens and lily pads went flying in all directions. "Oh, I just don't know what to do!"

"What's the matter? What's happened?" Nina asked, wide-eyed with worry.

"It's Madame Dupré. She's been taken ill very suddenly," Miss Meadowsweet explained, as she scrabbled around trying to pick everything up. "Doctor Leaf has arranged for her to go to hospital."

"Oh dear, I do hope she'll get better soon," Peri said, nervously chewing her fingernails.

"Yes." The secretary had gathered her belongings and was patting her hair anxiously. "The thing is, the timing is

terrible. As you know, Madame was going to organize a party for Miss Tremula. I just don't know if I can cope with running the Academy and planning a party without her."

Peri perked up. "We'll help!" she cried.

Bella nodded eagerly. "That's just what we were coming to say anyway," she said.

Miss Meadowsweet frowned. "I don't know . . . a party like this takes a lot of thought, and to tell you the truth I don't know where to start myself! I mean, I was only going to make a list of guests and send out the invitations. I'm not sure I have the faintest idea how to plan the entertainment. And then there's the catering—"

Peri interrupted before Miss Meadowsweet could get herself worked up again. "*We* can do all that!" she assured the secretary, her emerald eyes sparkling.

It was Nina's turn to object. "Hang on a second, Peri. It's a big job," she said. "I know we put on a show at the palace, but we had Queen Camellia's help then."

"We can do it," Peri persisted. "Listen, Miss Meadowsweet – you can still do the guest list and the invitations, I'll handle the food, and Nina and Bella would be great at organizing the entertainment. Bella, you must have loads of contacts through your mum and, Nina, you're brilliant at choreography. Trust me, guys. This party's going to be magic!"

Chapter Two

The bluebell rang for ballet classes, and the fairy ballerinas hurried along to their studio in silence. They arrived to find a stranger standing by the piano, talking to Miss Tremula. He was only a little taller than their teacher, but much younger. He had very short, cropped black hair and was wearing a leotard, white tights and black demi-pointe ballet shoes. He was handsome, with a dazzling smile that seemed to radiate white sparks, and he looked incredibly fit.

7

And scary, thought Nina. I wonder who he is?

This question was immediately answered by Miss Tremula, who welcomed her class, beaming.

"Good morning, fairies! I know that

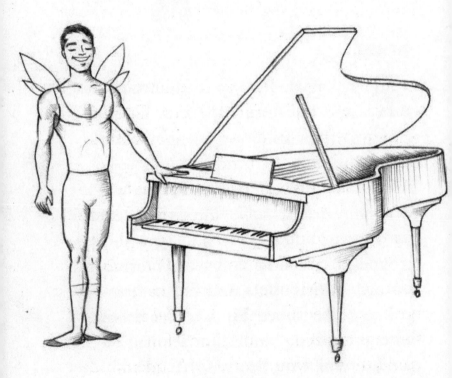

by now you will have heard the bad
news about Madame. But please do not
worry yourselves, dears. I am told that
she is in very good hands at the hospital.
And I know that she will want us to
carry on as normal with our lessons."

The class murmured, "Yes, Miss
Tremula," and shuffled uneasily. Everyone
was worried about Madame Dupré.

"And now for some good news," Miss
Tremula continued. "Let me introduce
our visitor . . . Monsieur Pierre Choux!"

The fairies eyed the stranger with
interest.

"What's his name? Something Shoe?"
whispered Peri, causing the fairies around
her to start giggling.

Miss Tremula frowned at Peri and
continued. "Monsieur Choux, as you will
have gathered from his *delightful* name,"
she emphasized, "is a French fairy. He has
come all the way from the Académie de
la Danse, where our own Madame Dupré

was a pupil. And he's kindly agreed to help us until we can find a permanent replacement for me when I retire."

I hope he speaks English as beautifully as Madame, thought Nina, or we'll never understand him.

"*Bonjour la classe!*" said Monsieur Choux seriously.

Nina's jaw dropped in horror. He doesn't speak any English at all! she thought.

Monsieur Choux smiled mischievously at Miss Tremula, his white teeth glittering brilliantly, then both teachers burst out laughing.

"It's all right, I do speak English as well," the new teacher said. "*Oh là là!* The look on your faces! Priceless!"

The class breathed a collective sigh of relief.

"I am very honoured to be at the Royal Academy of Fairy Ballet," Monsieur Choux said. "And it is delightful

to see so many beautiful English roses here," he continued, turning his gleaming smile on Bella.

At this, Bella immediately blushed and started fluttering her wings at the new teacher.

"Monsieur Choux is particularly interested in your pointe work," Miss Tremula explained.

"Indeed," said Monsieur Choux. "I wonder, Miss Tremula, could I observe some now?"

Peri looked at Nina nervously. The pointe work that Miss Tremula had shown them last term had been so hard. They had done endless exercises to strengthen their feet and toes, and Peri had found it very difficult.

Bella wasn't concerned though; she was already hurrying to the barre, eager to show off to her enchanting new teacher.

Chapter Three

onsieur Choux watched everything very carefully with beady eyes, and made notes in a glittery little lily pad with a tiny silver pen. The lesson was exhausting: the new teacher was certainly making sure that Miss Tremula showed him *everything* the fairy ballerinas had learned!

Over and over again they went through all the basic exercises they had done since arriving at the Academy. Then, instead of stopping for breaktime, Monsieur Choux insisted that the

ballerinas show him the demanding relevés on to demi-pointe that Miss Tremula had taught them.

Next Monsieur Choux wanted to test the fairies' sense of rhythm. So Miss Tremula asked them to do an exercise to display this skill, even though it was plain many of them were by now dropping on their feet.

"I would like you to show Monsieur Choux a 'battement tendu jeté'," said Miss Tremula. "Nina, perhaps you would care to demonstrate. Start in second position, please."

Frankly this was the last thing Nina felt like doing but, as ever, she wanted to please Miss Tremula. She held on to the barre with her left hand and shakily pointed her right foot out to the side. She was so tired.

"Can anyone remember the full name for this position?" Miss Tremula called out to the class.

Bella shot
her hand up in
the air, a look of
eager desperation
on her face.

"Yes?" said Miss
Tremula, trying to
hide a smile. She had
never seen Bella look so
keen to impress before.

Bella called out
primly: "It is called
a 'battement tendu
à la seconde'."

The rest of the class
looked baffled by this
answer: Bella had rather
overdone the French
accent in an obvious
effort to get Monsieur Choux's attention.
It seemed to do the trick, however, for the
new teacher clapped his hands and called
out, "Bravo!" flashing her an extra-huge

grin that showed off every one of his sparkling white teeth.

"That's right, dear," said Miss Tremula. "Now, Nina, if you're ready, Mrs Wisteria will play some appropriate music, and you will show us the battement tendu jeté, making sure you keep to the beat."

Nina pulled her shoulders back bravely, raised her right arm, her hand soft, and began throwing her right leg just a few centimetres off the ground in time with the music. But she was only able to complete five or six little bounces: Monsieur Choux's face turned redder and redder with each movement of Nina's foot. Then, looking as though he were on the point of exploding, he cried, "Stop! Stop the music!"

"W-what is it, Monsieur?" Nina asked anxiously.

"It was *far* too heavy," the new teacher shouted sharply. "The whole

point of the exercise is to demonstrate energy and lightness of touch! You move like one of your school puddings!"

Nina was flabbergasted. None of the teachers at the Academy had ever been so unkind to her. Miss Tremula always made the class work hard, but she never humiliated them like this.

Monsieur Choux turned to Bella and gave her another dazzling smile. "You, *mademoiselle* – what is your name?"

"Bella."

"Well, Bella," said Monsieur Choux, "please show the class how it should be done."

Bella blushed a deep shade of pink, then, taking Mrs Wisteria's lead, she started a series of battements tendus jetés. She kept her neck long and graceful and her back stretched and extended. Her left leg was strong and firm and did not move at all, while her right leg seemed to do all the work. With each beat of the dainty music, Bella raised and lowered her right leg in a series of delicate little pulses – up, down, up, down, up, down. She looked as though she were fluttering in mid-air rather than doing some exercises at the barre.

Bella's certainly on top form today, thought Nina enviously. She would

make a perfect prima ballerina. Monsieur Choux really is bringing out the best in her.

Monsieur Choux turned to Miss Tremula as if she had already retired and he had taken charge of her class. "Now *that*, I think you will agree," he said smugly, "is how it should be done."

Chapter Four

At long last the ballet class was dismissed. Bella immediately rushed over to the new teacher, who beamed delightedly at her. The pair were soon engaged in animated conversation, while Bella's exhausted friends drifted to the Refectory. They helped themselves to some sesame-seed buns and flopped down, wings drooping.

Bella buzzed up to her friends a little later, bubbling over with enthusiasm. "I had *such* a great chat with Monsieur just now," she gushed. "He told me all about his glittering career! He's even been to Russia! Imagine that . . ." Her almond-shaped eyes glistened and she sighed dramatically.

Nina frowned. "I don't know why you're so excited, Bella. I bet your mum's been to just as many wonderful places, hasn't she? Come to that, I'm sure Madame Dupré has too. She just doesn't show off about it."

"Oooh!" Bella jeered. "Who's a teensy-weensy bit jealous?"

Nina was taken aback. Bella hadn't shown off like this since her first day at the Academy. "What *are* you going on about?" she asked angrily.

"Oh, come on!" Bella retorted.

"You're just upset that he preferred my dancing to yours." She pirouetted showily and looked around to see if anyone was watching her.

Peri burst out laughing, spraying Bella with seeds and crumbs. "Hey, Nina, I think Bella's in *lurve!*"

"Am not!" Bella shouted crossly, brushing the mess from her leotard.

Nina was laughing too now, despite her tiredness. "Are too!" she squeaked.

Bella simply snorted and flew off in a huff.

Peri and Nina took their time flying

back to class. Despite being fed up with Bella, Nina was beginning to get worried that they had upset her.

"We'll have to apologize," she said. "We don't want Bella to be in a mood with us. We're supposed to be organizing the leaving party together, remember?"

Peri was still tittering quietly to herself. "I'm sorry. But you must admit, Bella *was* funny!" she said. "Fluttering her wings and looking at Monsieur Choux so adoringly! He's got her completely under his spell."

Nina couldn't help grinning at the memory. "I know," she agreed. "He's gross! Urgh, that awful toothy grin. I can't understand why she likes him so much. But still, we shouldn't tease her."

"Yes, you're right," Peri said, trying to keep a straight face. "But imagine if they got married – she'd be Bella 'Shoe' instead of Bella Glove!" The little imp creased up with laughter again.

Nina groaned. "That's *such* a bad joke," she said. "You've been spending far too much time with my sister." Nina's sister, Poppy, was always making similar cheesy remarks.

Peri stuck out her tongue playfully at her friend and whizzed ahead of her, shouting over her shoulder: "So what? Choux's a stupid name. You know it means 'cabbages', don't you! I looked it up in the dictionary. Hee hee! Maybe we should call Bella 'Mrs Cabbages'!"

Nina sighed and flew after her friend. I hope Peri doesn't say anything else to annoy Bella today, she thought.

When the fairy ballerinas returned to the studio they found Monsieur Choux already there. Miss Tremula had not yet arrived.

Nina and Peri took their places at the barre with their classmates and began a few stretches. Nina was just beginning

to wonder where Bella was when she zoomed in.

The new teacher rushed towards her at once in a whirlwind, his teeth dazzling.

"Ah, Bella, *la belle!*" he said dramatically.

Bella looked coyly at the floor and

fiddled with her hairclips. Nina tried not
to catch Peri's eye, as she felt sure her
friend would make another joke at Bella's
expense.

"Listen, everyone," announced
Monsieur Choux, clapping his hands. "I
have an announcement. As you all saw,
I was so impressed
with Bella's
beautiful
performance
this morning.
So, after class
I asked Bella
if she would
do me the
honour of
working
with me
on a dance
for Miss
Tremula's
party."

Bella looked up at
her friends and
beamed proudly.

"It will
be truly
fabulous!"
cried Monsieur
Choux. "But
fairies, not a
word to Miss
Tremula about this!"

Nina forced a
smile, but she was
annoyed to find
herself feeling a little
bit jealous as she
watched her friend
go over to chat with
the new teacher while
they waited for Miss
Tremula.

Chapter Five

he next few days passed in an endless routine of exhausting lessons. Monsieur Choux kept pressing Miss Tremula to push the fairy ballerinas harder and harder, and then after lessons he and Bella swanned off to practise her secret dance.

"Monsieur Choux has ruined everything!" Nina wailed, slumped on the window seat in their room on Charlock corridor.

"If it's Bella you're worried about, I'm sure you'll manage without her for a while," Peri muttered sourly. "She obviously couldn't wait to get away from us."

"Oh, Peri!" Nina cried, exasperated. "Of course I can't manage without her. We were going to plan the entertainment *together*. But we've not had a chance to discuss it, and now she's doing this solo in secret! How am I supposed to organize the rest of the show if I don't even know what Bella's dance will be like?" Nina was in a state; her usually smooth blonde hair was ruffled.

"Oh yeah – see what you mean," Peri said, frowning. Then she brightened as an idea came to her: "How about we put on a play instead? I could send for Willow

Shakespindle by grasshopper express – he could lend us some actors from his stage school . . ."

"I think the entertainment should have something to do with *dance*, don't you?" Nina said sharply. "Miss Tremula is our *ballet* teacher, after all," she reminded her friend. Peri was always going on about her actor friends.

Peri looked crushed. "All right, Nina. Well, if you're going to be so moody, perhaps you can come up with a better idea yourself. I'm going to sort out the food – that's my job, isn't it?" She whizzed out before Nina could apologize.

Nina fluttered distractedly around her bedroom, stopping every so often to gaze out of the little round window that looked over the wild-flower meadow.

Thinking of the choreography on my own is hard enough, she mused glumly, but how am I going to cope with organizing the costumes, decorations

and lighting too? My mind's a complete
blank. If only Bella would forget
Monsieur Choux and come and help me
– she's the social butterfly!

As if mirroring her thoughts, a
bright red butterfly suddenly appeared
in the meadow. It was chasing a
yellow butterfly in and out
of some cornflowers. The
creatures wove
gracefully
in between
the flowers,
flitting away
from each
other and
then
coming
together
again – it looked to
Nina as if they were
talking to one another.

Or dancing, she thought.

"That's it!" Nina cried aloud, landing with a bump on the window seat. "I'll plan a butterfly dance! I'll get a group of us to practise all the moves we've learned so far – all that demi-pointe work will be put to good use. And a butterfly costume should be easy – we've got our own wings, after all! Stuff Bella and Mr Stinky Cabbage. They can do their own thing."

Carried away with her ideas, Nina forgot her tiredness and whizzed off straight away to fetch her friends Nyssa Bean and Hazel Leafbud.

While Nina was getting her wings in a twist about her dance, Peri went to find Basil the chef to help her plan a menu. When she reached the kitchens, she found Basil in a flap, which was quite out of character. He was flying back and forth over a pile of parcels and packages, muttering madly to himself and ticking off a long list on his clipboard.

"Herb teas, croissants, fresh fruit, pâté . . ."

"Hi, Basil. What's up? You look like you're in a right stew – ha ha!" Peri chuckled.

"Oh, hiya, Periwinkle. No time to stop," the chef answered, too hassled to notice Peri's bad joke. "Must get all this to that Monsieur Choux's room. This delivery has just arrived for him from France. He doesn't think much of *my* cooking apparently," he said irritably as he filled three baskets that were lined up on the table.

"Right," Peri said. She gritted her teeth at the mention of the troublesome new teacher, but thought better of making any comment. The menu for the party was the most pressing item on Peri's agenda at the moment. "Basil, I need to talk to you about this party—"

"Having another of your midnight feasts, are you?" Basil interrupted. "Lovely jubbly! I haven't got time to discuss it, so you just help yourself. But you know I like a tidy kitchen, so DON'T make a mess!" And with that, he was off.

Chapter Six

"What in all enchantment am I going to do with this lot?" Peri said out loud as she stared up at the rows and rows of packets, tins and gleaming pots and pans. "I'm no cook. I've always had help before. And these recipes are far too complicated," she groaned as she leafed through some of Basil's books. She sat down abruptly on a kitchen toadstool and ruffled her spiky red hair anxiously.

Eventually she came to a decision. "I know Nina won't like this," she said to herself reluctantly, "but I'm going to have

to cast a little spell. Just a small one . . ."

She leaped off the toadstool and bravely waved her wand at the white wall in front of her, singing out:

> Magic powers, show to me
> An easy-peasy recipe
> For a chocolate birthday cake:
> Something even I could make!

At once a list of ingredients and some instructions appeared on the wall. The glittering writing spelled out a recipe for "A Chocolate Brownie Tower Cake". Next to it was a picture of a delicious-looking mountain of chocolate squares, each decorated with the name of one of Miss Tremula's pupils. There were one hundred gold candles on the tower, and Miss Tremula's name was spelled out on the top in hundreds and thousands.

Peri blanched. "Not sure I'll manage the decorations," she said aloud. "Oh well, at least I can have a go at making the brownies."

She began reading the instructions carefully. " 'Chocolate, flour, quail's eggs, sugar, butter . . . First, melt the butter and chocolate together . . .' This looks easy enough!" she told herself cheerfully.

Peri set to work melting some chocolate bars with the butter. "That was simple! A piece of fairy cake in fact – ho ho!" Peri congratulated herself. She measured out the flour and the sugar, spilling much of it on to the table.

"What next? Oh yes, quail's eggs. Hmm. How am I going to mix them in?"

she thought, turning the smooth objects over in her hands. "Oh well, here goes . . ." and so saying, she dropped the tiny speckled eggs, shells and all, directly into the brownie mixture. The eggs plopped in, sending gloopy lumps of chocolate flying out of the bowl. Then she added the flour and sugar and some chocolate drops: "to make it extra-chocolatey!" Peri said with glee.

By this time, there was flour and sugar everywhere, and blobs of chocolate littered the floor. Peri didn't notice this;

she was more interested in finishing her creation. She peered into the bowl. The mixture did look strangely bumpy, but Peri confidently scooped it into a baking tray, then, remembering to put on some oven gloves, she gingerly placed the tray in the hot oven. As she did this, the recipe faded and disappeared.

Basil's oven was a state-of-the-art model, built with a fairy timer, which meant that his food cooked in the beat of a butterfly's wing. So it was a matter of seconds before the kitchen was filled with the appetizing aroma of cooked chocolate.

PING! The fairy timer sounded, and Peri zoomed over with her oven gloves at the ready to get her cakes out.

At that moment Basil buzzed back into the kitchen. "Cor, what a gorgeous smell!" he cried. "Let's have a butcher's."

"Go for it," Peri said proudly.

Basil took a knife and sliced the

brownies. He lifted out a piece to sample.

"Bleurgh!" he spluttered, spitting out chocolate crumbs all over the tabletop. "What in the name of enchantment—?"

"Er, you don't like it?" Peri asked, jumping back in shock.

"What have you *done*, Periwinkle?" Basil shouted. "This is GROSS! There's eggshell in here!" he exclaimed, pulling a face.

"The recipe said to put eggs in," Peri said, feeling rather indignant.

"Not in their *shells*!" Basil cried in exasperation. "You are supposed to break the eggs *into*

the mixture and throw *away* the shells.
You silly little pixie!" Basil bellowed.
Then suddenly he noticed the mess Peri
had made. "And *look* at this. You're not
working in my kitchen ever again!"

Chapter Seven

While Peri was covered from wingtips to toe in chocolate mess, Nina was back in her room, struggling to get her other fairy friends to dance. At first Nyssa and Hazel had been delighted to be involved in planning the party.

"A butterfly dance is, like, so cool!" Hazel gushed.

"Thanks, Hazel," Nina said, smiling. "But, remember, it has to be a surprise for Miss Tremula. I don't want Holly Nightshade and the other First Years to hear about it, all right?"

The friends nodded and promised to keep the secret.

"Let's get started then," said Nina hurriedly. "Why don't we begin with a 'pas echappé' to make it look as if we are taking off into the air, like this."

Nina went into a perfect demi-plié in fifth position, her left leg tucked neatly behind her right with her left toe touching her right heel. Then she sprang lightly on to demi-pointe in second position, her arms held gracefully above her head.

Hazel and Nyssa placed their feet in fifth position, poised to copy their friend. "Hang on a minute," Nina called out.

"What's the matter?" Nyssa said.

"Your left toe isn't touching your right heel, Nyss," Nina said. "You've got to start properly or Miss T will notice."

Nyssa sighed noisily and corrected the position of her feet. The three fairies then leaped up on to their demi-pointe.

"Ouch!" Hazel cried, clutching her

right ankle. "I think I've overdone it in class this week, Nina. Sorry," she added, seeing the look of disappointment on Nina's face.

Nyssa was tired and grumpy too; Monsieur Choux's difficult ballet classes had taken their toll on her as well. "Look," she said stroppily, "we're fairies, so why can't we just *fly* if we're going to pretend to be butterflies?"

"Because we're not any old fairies, we're fairy ballerinas," Nina said, "and anyway, Miss Tremula wouldn't like it."

"'Miss Tremula wouldn't like it,'" Nyssa copied in a sing-song voice. "Oh frogspawn! You are so boring sometimes, Nina," she cried. "I'm sorry, but this isn't going to work. I've done enough demi-pointe work this week to finish me off, and I'm not doing any more, party or no party." And with a flick of her ponytail, she flounced out.

"This is a nightmare, Hazel!" Nina

cried. "There really will be 'no party' at this rate."

Hazel sighed, then her eyes lit up. "Listen, Nina. Why don't we use some magic to help us? Surely this counts as an emergency?"

Nina hesitated. It was a very tempting idea. But then she shook her head. "No, Hazel. I can't break the Number One Fairy Rule. Madame would never forgive me."

Hazel smiled weakly and patted her friend on the shoulder. "You're probably right," she agreed. "Well, don't worry, Nina. At least Peri's going to cook some yummy food."

"No, I'm not!" came a tortured wail. Peri crashed through the door, still covered in cake mixture. She had been crying, and rivers of chocolate were streaming down her cheeks. The sight was so comical that Nina began to giggle. Unfortunately this made

Peri cry even harder. Hazel tactfully went off to find Nyssa, leaving Nina to calm Peri down as she explained the kitchen catastrophe in between her sobs. "Basil said he'd never let me in his kitchen again." Peri gave a long, shuddering sigh. What are we going to do?"

You know, I think Hazel was right," Nina said grimly, "I never thought I'd say this, but I'm going to have to use a little magic . . ."

Chapter Eight

"What?" Peri gasped. "Nina! You've *never* used magic at the Academy before. You've always disapproved of it when Bella or I have tried."

Nina nodded. "I know," she said. "But this *is* an emergency." She gritted her teeth, closed her eyes and held out her wand stiffly in front of her. Quietly but purposefully she began to chant:

Fairy Magic, we're in a mess.
Help us out of our distress!
We know it is against the rule

To employ magic in our school,
But we are desperate today.
We really need to find a way
To organize a party quick.
(Madame can't help us, she is sick.)
Please bring us food that is delicious
(Basil must not be suspicious).
We also need to plan a dance!
This is our last and only chance
To plan out every single feature
Of a party for our teacher.

WHIZZ! BANG! ZAP!
Golden-yellow stars,
flowers and hearts shot
out of Nina's wand and filled
the little bedroom. The fairy

friends tingled all over their tiny bodies, and Peri yelped in fear.

"What have you done, Nina?" she cried. "That must have been some spell!"

"It certainly was!" said a voice.

The colourful shapes faded and the fairies turned to face the speaker, who was hovering in the doorway. She was dressed in a bright yellow suit and she looked very neat and smart. She was wearing small glasses that perched on the end of her nose and was carrying a yellow briefcase. She fluttered in busily, seemingly

unaware of the looks on the fairy friends'
faces. Nina and Peri almost fainted with
shock.

"Wh-wh-who are you?" Nina
managed at last.

"Don't you know? You should do
– *you* conjured me up!" said the yellow
fairy wryly. "You said you wanted
a party? Well, you've got one: I am
Primrose Perfect, of Perfect Party Planet,"
she announced in a clipped, efficient tone.

"Wow!" Peri breathed. "You come
from a different planet?"

"Er, no," Primrose replied slowly.
"I organize parties for busy fairies who
haven't the time to do it themselves. My
business is called Perfect Party Planet," she
explained impatiently.

"Oh, I – I see," Peri said,
embarrassed.

"We Aim to Please by Providing the
Pinnacle of Party Perfection!" Primrose
said as if quoting from a brochure.

"Looks like you've come just in time then!" cried Nina.

Primrose Perfect made Nina and Peri tell her why they were in such a panic, and the two fairies gratefully unburdened themselves of all their worries. Nina even told Primrose all about Bella's new-found friendship with Monsieur Choux. She was surprised to find herself confessing how jealous she was that her friend was getting so much special attention from the new teacher.

"I'm – I'm sorry, Primrose," Nina said at last, feeling rather ashamed of herself. "I don't know why I've told you all that."

Primrose smiled kindly. "No need to apologize, dear," she said briskly. "You'd be surprised at the things I get told in my line of work. Now, first things first. What sort of a theme were you thinking of? What's that you've got there, Periwinkle?"

Peri had been quietly doodling on a piece of paper while Nina poured her heart out to Primrose. "Oh, I – I was just making a list of the food we could have," she said shyly.

Primrose took the paper and scanned it quickly. "There's an awful lot of chocolate here," she said critically.

There was a burst of laughter from the doorway. "That makes sense!" said a voice the friends recognized. "It's Peri's favourite food."

"Bella!" cried Peri.

"Good of you to turn up," said Nina sarcastically.

Bella's smile faded and she was about to snap back at her friend when Primrose stepped in quickly. "Good. We're all here then," she said cheerfully. "Let's get to work, shall we?"

Chapter Nine

"Who's this, Nina?" asked Bella. "Aren't you going to introduce me?"

Nina wasn't quite ready to forgive Bella. "This is Primrose Perfect," she hissed. "She's a party organizer. I had to break the Number One Rule and conjure her up to help us because a *certain fairy* flew off and left us in the lurch." Bella tried to protest, but Nina continued: "And she already knows all about you."

Bella looked stung. "Don't be mean," she whispered.

Nina snorted in disbelief. "Me, mean?" she cried. "You're the one who flew off into the sunset with Monsieur Choux and left me and Peri while you planned your wonderful *solo* dance—"

"I know I abandoned you, Nina, and I'm sorry, but I've had enough of that horrid Monsieur Choux. So I was hoping you'd forgive me and let me help you . . ."

Nina raised her eyebrows.

"It's true, Nina. He's worked me into the ground. He's never satisfied with anything I do and my legs and feet are killing me," Bella continued, starting to cry.

Nina softened at the sight of her friend sobbing and moved to put an arm around her. "OK. Sit down, Bella, and tell us all about it," she said.

Bella described the lessons she had been having with Monsieur Choux. The classes

had got harder and harder as the teacher forced her to try moves she wasn't ready for.

"He wanted me to do the splits!" she cried. "I thought my legs would burst, it was so painful."

Peri and Nina gasped.

"In the end I had to tell Miss Tremula how tough he's been and she agreed he's pushed us all too hard. She went to talk to him about it and apparently he flew

off the handle at her and said he'd never taught such a bunch of clumsy toads in his life before. So he's packed his bags and gone!"

"Does this mean you're too worn out to dance any more?" Nina asked worriedly.

"Probably," Bella sniffed. "I'm exhausted, and my feet are covered in blisters."

Nina looked at Peri, and Peri nodded, reading her friend's thoughts. Nina stood in front of Bella and pointed her wand at her. Then she said quietly:

Poor Bella's legs are tired and sore,
She feels that she can dance no more.
Come magic, take away the pain
And let's see Bella dance again!

A light sprinkling of violet glitter fell gently on to Bella's legs and a sweet smell of lavender filled the room. Bella

closed her eyes and smiled as if someone was giving her a relaxing massage.

"Ah," she said with feeling, "that's better."

But then her eyes snapped open as she realized what Nina had done.

"Nina Dewdrop!" she cried. "Did you just break the Number One Fairy Rule *again*?"

Nina laughed uncomfortably. "Yes, Bella Glove, I did."

"Come come, fairies," cut in Primrose. "We must knuckle down or there won't be a dance *or* a party."

The fairies were discussing possible themes for the party.

"Miss T loves wildlife," said Peri.

Primrose scribbled this down. "In that case, let's use your butterfly-dance idea, Nina," she said. "We could make the party room look like the wild-flower meadow—"

Bella agreed. "Miss Tremula loves relaxing in the meadow at the end of the day."

"What about a waterfall?" Primrose suggested.

"Yes!" said Nina excitedly. "In fact, instead of a waterfall, we could have an elderflower-fall!" she added.

"A what?" chorused the others.

"Follow me," said Nina. She fluttered into the bathroom and hovered by the bath, then she gave her wand a dramatic flourish and chanted:

A party drink from elderflowers
Cascading down in sparkling showers!

WHOOSH!
Peri and Primrose jumped back just in time to avoid being soaked. A waterfall of sparkling elderflower cordial was gushing out of the shower head into the

bath. Nina grabbed a tooth mug and
filled it with the magical liquid. She took
a large slug and grinned, wiping her
mouth on the back of her hand.

"Delicious!" she cried. And then
burped.

Primrose tutted, but Peri and Bella
burst out laughing.

"What's got into you, Nina
Dewdrop?" cried Bella. "First you do
not *one* magic spell but *three* – and now
you're burping!"

All three friends threw their arms
around each other, giggling, and
Primrose smiled.

Chapter Ten

ina, Peri, Bella and Primrose
worked their wings off preparing for
the party. With Primrose secretly helping,
Nina managed to persuade Nyssa, Hazel
and a few others to join in the dance.
Peri didn't want to perform. She stuck
to helping Primrose and making sure
that Miss Meadowsweet had sent out all
the invitations. Lots of Nina's classmates
were tired and sore after being worked so
hard by Monsieur Choux, and Nina cast
secret spells on all the fairies who were
struggling. She knew she was taking a

big risk, but everything *had* to be perfect for Miss Tremula's special day.

On the afternoon of the party, once everything was in place, Primrose quietly left the Academy, leaving Nina and her fairy friends in charge of the celebrations.

The magical evening started with some music from a small orchestra that Primrose had supplied. She had also arranged for some waiters. They were dressed as ladybirds, bumblebees, hummingbirds and damselflies, and hovered among the guests carrying platters of food. The drinks flowed from a cascading waterfall of refreshing, sparkling cordial. The rest of

the food seemed to serve itself – plates of delicious treats were tied to the bottom of cloud-shaped balloons that floated around the room. On the stage in the Grand Hall, a golden table had been placed. This was for the birthday cake – a tower of chocolate brownies with one hundred candles, decorated in tiny silver balls. Peri was delighted.

"You don't think we've gone over the top, do you?" Nina whispered.

"Are you joking?" Peri grinned. "This is mega! Trust me, Miss T will love it."

On the stroke of eight the music died down and everyone turned to face the doors. Miss Tremula appeared, wearing an elegant pale blue ballgown, her wispy silver hair piled high in an intricate style. The orchestra immediately struck up the first few notes of "Happy Birthday", and everyone sang loudly.

As she advanced,

the pupils of the Royal Academy of
Fairy Ballet stepped back into two lines,
forming a corridor for her to walk down.
She slowly made her way to the stage.
Much to her joy, Madame Dupré was
waiting for her. ("You didn't think I
would miss your party, did you?" she
whispered, winking. It appeared that the
headmistress was back on form.)

At once the music stepped up in
tempo and a whirl of colour rushed into
the centre of the room: Nyssa, Hazel
and five more Second Years were criss-
crossing over the floor of the hall, leaping
and twirling. They had never danced so
magnificently. They stopped in front of
Miss Tremula in a line so that the colours
of their costumes ranged from left to right
in the colours of the rainbow.

Then they drew back gracefully. A
flute called out silvery rippling notes that
mimicked sparkling river water – and
Nina and Bella appeared. Nina was

wearing a bright red leotard and tutu
and Bella was dressed in yellow. They
had strips of gossamer hanging from their
arms. Both the fairies wore hairbands
that had silver antennae attached to
them.

They look *exactly* like exotic butterflies,
Peri thought happily.

Nina and Bella danced in a pair, past
the rainbow, starting with a delicate skip.
Nina turned her head first to the left, then
to the right as her left foot stretched out
in front, then her right. Bella mirrored
her movements precisely. Their arms were
soft, their necks long, their backs straight:
Miss Tremula fought back the tears as she
gazed fondly at her pupils.

Then Bella stepped back and Nina
ran to stop in front of Miss Tremula and
went into an 'écarté derrière' – a delicate
pose where her left foot was turned out,
her right foot pointed beautifully to the
side, and her right arm held gracefully

above her head. She gently lifted her
right leg high behind her in an advanced
arabesque. Her back arched strongly: it
looked as if she were about to soar up
into the air and leave everyone
behind.

Nina looked up, beaming at
Miss Tremula. The music brightened,
and Nina leaped into a series of pas
de chats, lifting her left leg neatly behind
her and springing up on to demi-pointe
on her right foot. Then she spun round
and round, performing perfect fouettés,
her right leg propelling her at top speed.
She ended in fifth position, while Bella
and the others weaved around her like
flowers blowing in the wind.

The music ended with a flourish and
Bella scooped Nina up in a spectacular
lift. She was held firmly around her tiny
waist, and held her left arm softly in the
air as if waving goodbye to the audience.
Everyone gasped at this performance.

How had Bella learned to lift like that?
Surely she wasn't strong enough?

The audience rose to its feet, clapping,
cheering and whooping. The noise was
deafening! Nina had tears streaming
down her face as she looked across to
Miss Tremula and saw the look of pride
in the old fairy's eyes.

At last the applause died down and
Miss Tremula stood up, leaning heavily
on her cane.

"Thank you," she said quietly.
"Thank you so much for such a
magnificent party. I am overwhelmed
– you all know how difficult it is for me
to say goodbye. But at least I can leave
in the knowledge that there are many
talented ballerinas here, who will uphold
the good name of the Academy." She
faltered, and Madame Dupré kindly came
to her aid.

"I just want to add a few words of
thanks as well," she said. "I'm sorry that

I was not here to plan this party myself. But Nina, Bella and Periwinkle – you have managed very well without me!"

Nina blushed at this and tried to interrupt.

"It's all right, Nina dear. I can tell that you and your friends must have bent the Number One Fairy Rule to achieve all this—"

"Madame, I'm sorry—"

"But," the

headmistress continued, holding up her hand to silence Nina, "just this once, I think we can overlook it. After all, this wasn't just magic, was it?"

"No, Madame," answered Nina, beaming. "It was PARTY MAGIC!"

A selected list of titles available from Macmillan Children's Books

The prices shown below are correct at the time of going to press. However, Macmillan Publishers reserves the right to show new retail prices on covers, which may differ from those previously advertised.

ANNA WILSON

NINA FAIRY BALLERINA

New Girl	978-0-330-43985-5	£3.99
Daisy Shoes	978-0-330-43986-2	£3.99
Best Friends	978-0-330-43987-9	£3.99
Show Time	978-0-330-43988-6	£3.99
Flying Colours	978-0-330-44622-8	£3.99
Double Trouble	978-0-330-44620-4	£3.99
Party Magic	978-0-330-44778-2	£3.99
Dream Treat	978-0-330-44780-5	£3.99

All Pan Macmillan titles can be ordered from our website, www.panmacmillan.com, or from your local bookshop and are also available by post from:

Bookpost, PO Box 29, Douglas, Isle of Man IM99 1BQ
Credit cards accepted. For details:
Telephone: 01624 677237
Fax: 01624 670923
Email: bookshop@enterprise.net
www.bookpost.co.uk

Free postage and packing in the United Kingdom